ABOUT THE BANK STREET READY-TO-READ SERIES

Seventy years of educational research and innovative teaching have given the Bank Street College of Education the reputation as America's most trusted name in early childhood education.

Because no two children are exactly alike in their development, we have designed the *Bank Street Ready-to-Read* series in three levels to accommodate the individual stages of reading readiness of children ages four through eight.

- *Level 1*: GETTING READY TO READ—read-alouds for children who are taking their first steps toward reading.
- *Level 2*: READING TOGETHER—for children who are just beginning to read by themselves but may need a little help.
- *Level 3*: I CAN READ IT MYSELF—for children who can read independently.

Our three levels make it easy to select the books most appropriate for a child's development and enable him or her to grow with the series step by step. The *Bank Street Ready-to-Read* books also overlap and reinforce each other, further encouraging the reading process.

We feel that making reading fun and enjoyable is the single most important thing that you can do to help children become good readers. And we hope you'll be a part of Bank Street's long tradition of learning through sharing.

The Bank Street College of Education

For Bennett

−G.B.K.

For Jacob Harmon Lieberstein

−S.A.

WHO GOES OUT ON HALLOWEEN?
A Bantam Little Rooster Book

Simultaneous paper-over-board and trade paper editions/September 1990

Little Rooster is a trademark of Bantam Books,
a division of Bantam Doubleday Dell Publishing Group, Inc.

Special thanks to Betsy Gould and Erin B. Gathrid.

Library of Congress Cataloging-in-Publication Data

Alexander, Sue, 1933–
Who goes out on Halloween?

(Bank Street ready-to-read)
Summary: Enumerates the various creatures out on
Halloween, from fat monsters and pirates to small witches and ghosts.
[1. Halloween−Fiction.   2. Stories in rhyme].
I. Karas, G. Brian, ill.   II. Title. III. Series.
PZ8.3.A378Wh   1990   [E]   89-18468
ISBN 0-553-05891-6
ISBN 0-553-34922-8

Bantam Books are published by Bantam Books, a division of Bantam Doubleday Dell
Publishing Group, Inc. Its trademark, consisting of the words "Bantam Books" and
the portrayal of a rooster, is Registered in U.S. Patent and Trademark Office and in
other countries. Marca Registrada. Bantam Books, 666 Fifth Avenue, New York,
New York 10103.

PRINTED IN THE UNITED STATES OF AMERICA

0   9   8   7   6   5   4   3   2   1

Bank Street Ready-to-Read™

Who Goes Out on Halloween?

by Sue Alexander
Illustrated by G. Brian Karas

A BANTAM LITTLE ROOSTER BOOK

NEW YORK · TORONTO · LONDON · SYDNEY · AUCKLAND

Who goes out on Halloween?

Who climbs up steps?
Who knocks on doors?

Tall witches.
Small witches.

Any-size-   at-all witches.

Striped clowns.
Spotted clowns.

Even polka-dotted clowns.

And some mini-bunnies.

Who goes out on Halloween?

Any-size-at-all pirates.

Striped cats.
Spotted cats.

Even polka-dotted cats.

And some mini-monsters.

Space people go out
on Halloween.
See? Here they come!

Everyone goes out
on Halloween!

Witches and clowns walk side by side.

Bunnies and ghosts look
for places to hide.

Pirates and cats
walk in a row.

Monsters and space people
see who they know.

They go by twos
and threes and fours.
They climb up steps.
They knock on doors.
They hold out bags.

And then they say . . .